Absolute Power

Zapf Chancery Tertiary Level Publications

A Guide to Academic Writing by C. B. Peter (1994)

Africa in the 21st Century by Eric M. Aseka (1996)

Women in Development by Egara Kabaji (1997)

Introducing Social Science: A Guidebook by J. H. van Doorne (2000)

Elementary Statistics by J. H. van Doorne (2001)

Iteso Survival Rites on the Birth of Twins by Festus B. Omusolo (2001)

The Church in the New Millennium: Three Studies in the Acts of the Apostles by John Stott (2002)

Introduction to Philosophy in an African Perspective by Cletus N.Chukwu (2002)

Participatory Monitoring and Evaluation by Francis W. Mulwa and Simon N. Nguluu (2003)

Applied Ethics and HIV/AIDS in Africa by Cletus N. Chukwu (2003)

For God and Humanity: 100 Years of St. Paul's United Theological College Edited by Emily Onyango (2003)

Establishing and Managing School Libraries and Resource Centres by Margaret Makenzi and Raymond Ongus (2003)

Introduction to the Study of Religion by Nehemiah Nyaundi (2003)

A Guest in God's World: Memories of Madagascar by Patricia McGregor (2004)

Introduction to Critical Thinking by J. Kahiga Kiruki (2004)

Theological Education in Contemporary Africa edited by GrantLeMarquand and Joseph D. Galgalo (2004)

Looking Religion in the Eye edited by Kennedy Onkware (2004)

Computer Programming: Theory and Practice by Gerald Injendi (2005)

Demystifying Participatory Development by Francis W. Mulwa (2005)

Music Education in Kenya: A Historical Perspective by Hellen A. Odwar (2005)

Into the Sunshine: Integrating HIV/AIDS into Ethics Curriculum Edited by Charles Klagba and C. B. Peter (2005)

Integrating HIV/AIDS into Ethics Curriculum: Suggested Modules Edited by Charles Klagba (2005)

Dying Voice (An Anthropological Novel) by Andrew K. Tanui (2006)

Participatory Learning and Action (PLA): A Guide to Best Practice by Enoch Harun Opuka (2006)

Science and Human Values: Essays in Science, Religion, and Modern Ethical Issues edited by Nehemiah Nyaundi and Kennedy Onkware (2006)

Understanding Adolescent Behaviour by **Daniel Kasomo (2006)**

Students' Handbook for Guidance and Counselling by Daniel Kasomo (2007)

BusinessOrganization and Management: Questions and Answers by Musa O. Nyakora (2007)

Auditing Priniples: A Stuents' Handbook by Musa O. Nyakora (2007)

The Concept of Botho and HIV/AIDS in Botswana edite by Joseph B. R. Gaie and Sana K. MMolai (2007)

Captive of Fate: A Novel by Ketty Arucy (2007)

A Guide to Ethics by Joseph Njino (2008)

(Continued after Bibliography)

Absolute Power
(and other stories)

Ambrose Rotich Keitany

Zapf Chancery
Eldoret, Kenya

First Published 2009
© Ambrose Rotich Keitany

Cover Concept and Design
C. B. Peter

Associate Designer and Typesetter
Nancy Njeri

Editor and Publishing Consultant
C. B. Peter

Printed by
Kijabe Printing Press,
P. O. Box 40,
Kijabe.

Published by

Zapf Chancery Research Consultants and Publishers,
P. O. Box 4988,
Eldoret, Kenya.
Email: zapfchancerykenya@yahoo.co.uk
Mobile: 0721-222 311 or 0723 775 166

ISBN-10: 9966-7341-4-7
ISBN-13: 978-9966-7341-4-3

Content

Introduction

By Prof. Chris L. Wanjala,
Professor of Literature
University of Nairobi

Before you, are twelve short stories exploring aspects of the 21st Century life in the rural as well as urban African setting, and giving you a jolt on the bliss of courtship and the pain of maintaining a marriage. The themes cover a wide range—from the tenacity with which old demagogues hold onto political power, to teenage love and infatuation in the village setting; family life with its challenging and inexorable attraction of married men to their extra-marital satisfaction while their libidinal energy still lasts; and the pain that such wayward men bring to their wives and children.

Early in the anthology you will encounter vociferous sloganeering that accompanies political campaigns, the intense activities and vicissitudes of life concomitant with early childhood and growing up in Africa and the allure of Western life which is mistaken for a globalization which sweeps, like a bad whiff, through all the nooks and unprotected space in which men, women and children live. Vestiges of traditional life and practices preach that the girl child should grow up at the side of her mother within the range of firm watch of the extended family, thus subjecting her to forced child labour characterized by domestic chores and duties, whilst the boy child lazies around, cutting corners and breathlessly pursuing after the girl child as the latter wearily goes to the river, the well, or the local forest, in search of water and firewood for domestic use. A loose urchin escapes the less stringy hold of his father, and waylays the unsuspecting girl child at water points, and makes infatuated advances at her as he seeks to assuage his lust, couched in seductive allusions to "love."

We go back to E. M. Forster's suggestion that for a story to be interesting, the reader should discover "how things turn out". The reader knows his or her interest and that that interest is satisfied by features of the story. Most of the stories in this volume are told from the point of view of the youth, highlighting political violence over disputed election results or a usurped island in the middle of an African lake or ocean, and in all this drama the youth take leading roles. The reader will readily recognize the points of view and how the stories offered here are different and why the difference makes a difference. The short stories highlight unbridled rivalry which culminates in *coups d' etat,* and the incessant counterblasts among politicians of different ethnic groups and religious backgrounds. As it were, brother slays brother in the vicious and diabolical power struggle. Rural stories in this anthology tell you what you should do when your village, or your community, is attacked by voracious swarms of locusts which ravage the green stretches of your countryside and turn them into desiccated brown patches. These are hitherto unsung calamities that compare with earthquakes that have rocked South-East Asia, the floods which have visited Americans in New Orleans, and the Tsunamis of ocean waters. One feels in these accounts that the world is definitely coming to an end. Some of these short stories read like reports in high noon on events in villages; they capture the goings-on in the lives of peasants and nomadic pastoralists of our time. The book ends with stories about adult life of marriage that would prepare a young reader of short fiction for the elaborate accounts of romance and infidelity in George Eliot's *Middlemarch* and Flaubert's *Emma Bovary*. The accounts in this book take our mind's eye to alien locales and distant climes.

The stories do not only invite the reader to assume the feelings, voices, and postures of the narrator and characters, but also offer varying tastes in stylistic, structural, characterizing, and thematic aspects, suited to all educational levels of our country. Undergraduates in our universities will be fascinated by the symbols and allusions, the descriptive detail, nuance, and the sense of pattern of imagery, that give unity to the stories in the last quarter of the anthology. The mature reader will come across deliberate structural devices like foreshadowing and flashback which reveal themselves. Thematic units like survival and initiation are in the anthology, especially in its initial pages. The short stories portray the countryside as un-spoilt; the countryside is the setting of rituals like circumcision and what western donors call "Female Genital Mutilation".

In these short stories, which are almost wholly narrative with little or no dialogue, we encounter a setting where the most sophisticated machines are the power saws which deafen the peasants' ears as they fell age-old trees leading to desertification. This anthology records sounds very well. Besides the "tick-tock tick-tock of the clock in *The Seed of Evil*, we have "Ding! Dong! Ding! Dong!" of the church bells in the rural setting. The cockcrow can be heard at the wee hours of the night. It is described as "the unfailing alarm which wakes villages by four thirty". The stories show that if there are any motor vehicles in the rural areas at all, they are one car, probably a land rover.

The school and the church are a novelty. The youth in school are a spectacle to watch. The short fiction in this anthology reminds the sexagenarian reader of *Buniongo* or the fagging that went on in secondary schools when Form I students arrived as "freshers". A fag (formerly British) was a young public school boy who, according to *Collins Paperback English Dictionary* performed menial chores for an older boy. A fagged newcomer to a secondary school is referred to in this anthology as "a rabble".

There is a vicious struggle between the old and the new in the African continent. But it would be naïve to the extreme if we reduced characters in the plotted short stories to establishing conflict at their points of crisis as culture conflict. The African-Western dichotomy in terms of conflicting world views becomes simplistic—especially as we see it in Ngugi's trilogy (*The River Between*; *Weep Not, Child;* and *A Grain of Wheat*) and Chinua Achebe's tetralogy of early novels (*Things Fall Apart*; *No Longer at Ease*; *Arrow of God* and *A Man of the People)*. We should reduce the subject of conflict to characterization and identify the points of crisis that ensue in the individual story. My interest here regarding the two short stories; *Kidnapped*, and *Torn Asunder*, is how the stories can be of genuine intellectual interest. The first short story is written in the tragic mode whilst the latter is written in the mode of comedy in the Shakespearean sense. How else do you explain a runaway husband returning to his wife?

In this anthology, the suicide note left behind by Stephano Chumo is entitled, *An Epistle of the Departed*. The author of the note commits suicide because of the scare of traditions which stand in the way of the individual who wants to be free and separated from the enslaving and barbaric cultural practices. The irony in the suicidal note is in the victim's prayer that "God the Almighty Father rests my soul in eternal peace." Would God approve of suicide even in the circumstances of the protagonist?

Characters in the book are drunks, coup leaders, secondary school students, brides and grooms, and even, symbolically locusts and snakes. Despite the weaknesses of these characters, the stories about them teach moral lessons. A snake is a beautiful and dangerous reptile to behold. The stories portray the egotistic tendencies of political dictators and the tendency among modern rulers who resist change because they want the *status quo* to prevail for the benefit of the immediate members of their families and their tribes.

Fiction in general belongs to traditions and literary modes left by the masters like Hawthorne, Poe, De Maupassant, Anton Chekhov and J.D. Saligner, to mention but a few. The more highbrow prose writers are James Joyce, D. H. Lawrence and George Eliot. In Africa, the deft short story writers are Grace Ogot, Alex la Guma, Bessie Head and Dambudzo Marechera. As I read the short stories in this anthology, I wanted to know whether or not they added to my knowledge of the short story as a form. Some of the short stories in the book are episodes in the sense that they dealt with one or two events. The reader will deconstruct them and add something to them.

Dialogue is a scarce commodity in the early part of the book. In a way, the earlier part of the book draws a lot from the African oral tradition where the narrator dominates the movement of the story. In modern narratives, however, dialogue, conversation between two people, and discussions among many people, add drama and décor to a story. This is best illustrated by *Kidnapped*, *A Glimpse of the Deity*, and *Torn Asunder*. The lexical world in the earlier stories in the anthology include words in African languages. In *Torn Asunder*, the use of *Boerewoers* (A South African traditional home made farmer's sausage) shows that Afrikaans words can be adopted to enrich the English language. Elsewhere we see how Kiswahili words act as loan words in English texts.

There is something for every reader in this book. The young will find something to interest them. The youth will find the subject about urban life and the new Western education interesting. Those adults who have grown up on the novels and short stories of John Updike will appreciate reading something about the family, an excellent alternative to one of his latest, *Seek My Face*. This anthology proves that crime fiction with violence, love, death, and fast action, is here and now, and that it must be discussed in our lecture halls and the living rooms of our homes.

JEMATIA'S DAY

*Kolwon ng'o mbere nyo nemi chebaren...Taburolanga
chesaina.*
Who will cultivate my land at chebaren ... Chesaina,
he with a silk shirt.

It is half past seven in the morning but Komen is
already high after taking two litres of *Kiprewon*, the
early morning drink. His lament on who should
cultivate for him his land at Chebaren is a regular tune
heard when Jematia is serving the rest of the family
with tea and pancakes.

Not long after swallowing the delicious meal,
Jematia's elder brothers fizzle in the direction of
Kamesien, the town centre where the lazy youth loiter
about playing snooker, darts, cards and other games
known for converting rich men of the past to paupers
of today. Thirty minutes later, the whole of Jematia's
home becomes deserted except for Kobilo, Jematia's
mother and one Kop Jebet, a poor casual laborer ready
to offer a hand in sowing maize seeds in a bid to get a
meal for herself and her grandchildren.

Chiip...chiip...chiip...chiip... Jematia the teenage girl
of about fifteen calls the chickens as she throws around
bits of the leftover *ugali*. After the chickens are well
fed, as noted by the kingly cock's dramatization of
stretching the right leg and describing a circle around
a satisfied hen accompanied by masochistic sounds,

Jematia gets the maize seeds from the grass-thatched silo. For the next five hours, the three women will be toiling, planting maize and beans on the sloppy farm. Jematia's specific roles will include collecting the cow-dung manure and putting it in the seed holes and occasionally rushing home to add water to the *githeri* on the fireplace.

The farm work comes to halt when the sun is well above the laborer's heads and the planters' shadows are invisible. The young girl is expected to accompany Kipkoros to the river so as to be sure the four cows have drunk water, otherwise Kipkoros will return them halfway as he busies himself hunting wild birds with his treasured catapult.

The girl's role does not end there; the beautiful girl embarks on cleaning utensils and collecting leaves so as to make the compound tidier. Her efficiency in cleaning the compound is hampered by the crying toddler left yesterday by the teenage girl impregnated by Kipsang, Jematia's older brother. Soothing the toddler proves an uphill task and Jematia has to forever sing a lullaby until her voice goes sour.

To ensure the young baby falls into deep sleep, Jematia has to spend the next fifteen minutes in bed with the young one but the sweet dutiful rest is cut short by a quick reminder by her mother that she has to collect firewood from the steepy Kibele bush as she herself begins the journey of going to grind millet at the far home of Shokwei, the only household with a hand mill. Not long after Jematia and Jemator, her neighbor, have collected firewood, one sly boy known for making noise in school emerges from the bush and with genuine pretence asks for his lost she-goat. Despite being informed by the girls of their lack of knowledge on the said goat, Koigoi finds himself not leaving the place. After a few wry smiles accompanied by continuous kicking of a nearby stump, Koigoi tells Jematia of his long time desire to have her close to his chest

"Jematia, You know that you are very beautiful and a shining star. I really love you and want you very much. Do you love me? I think of you all the time, I cant even eat," the sophomore in the nearby secondary school concludes his amateurish wooing of Jematia. Within a short while, Jematia and Jemator are ready with a back full of firewood thanks to the lad who in that short time had helped in dissecting the hardwood branch into shiny firewood. The light-skinned form two student dressed in school pullover though it is a weekend, bids the girls farewell with high hopes that tomorrow will come with luck.

Upon arrival from the bushes, Jematia has to hurriedly clean the "Treetop" bottle and run fast to Soi's place for milk. The scantily dressed girl arrives home safely after a close shave with the devil. The stiff scared Jematia narrates to her Mum how she escaped the evil intentions of Kipring, the bully. Kipring had dragged her to the bush. Were it not for Kukop Zeddy who was attending a biological function in the same bush, Jematia would have been converted into the family way. Her mum makes moving apologies to her daughter and together they go into a short prayer accompanied by a few curses on Kipring.

As her father seats comfortably in the main house enjoying a cup of tea and listening on the small wireless Voice of Kenya and BBC London, the now fatigued girl has to read at least for a while and do the Maths and English assignments as her mother prepares supper for the whole family. So tired is Jematia that the delicious meal of *Sakchan,* *Mursik* and millet *Ugali* hardly make her appetite.

Her dreams in slumber-land are cut short at about three in the morning when Mother wakes her up to accompany her to Tirlenjun stream to fetch water. Water has to be fetched and put in a drum at such impossible hours because it is dry season and come daylight there would be a mile of jerry cans waiting to be filled. Slowly Jematia wakes up and remembers to be vigilant today to avoid the spitting cobra she encountered yester night.

The early morning finds Jematia smarting herself in preparation to teach the little boys and girls in the nearby Sunday school. After teaching the young ones on the importance of obeying one's parents as the holy book says in Ephesians 6:1and Philippians 4:4 Jematia leads the forty plus children of God in singing the choruses *"Mowechikei Awendi Misri"* and *"Tos Ngo ne Yoe Arawet?*

Ten thirty finds Jematia, Jemutai and Jebichii at the distant Nyoker River washing a load of laundry including seat covers, blankets, school uniforms and the priceless Christmas clothes. It is by this stream that other idiots of the male species by the names Kipchumba, Kimalit and Kisolit offer entertainment in the form of seduction to the busy girls. The young men who had just left their cows starving in the cowshed are reminded by one intelligent boy that they were the last in the mid year exams while Jemosop was number one despite their well-to-do background. The now ashamed trio excuse themselves but asks for an opportunity to meet them later in the day. Just then, Jematia asks her friends to quickly do the washing so that they may kindly assist her in smearing her brothers' cottage. Kipchumba, one of Jematia's elder brothers had politely commanded Jematia to ensure his *Siroino* was smeared and a kettleful of tea and a number of doughnuts were availed to him by three in the afternoon.

After neatly packing the laundry, the girls walk downstream to take a bath. It is there that the girls, right to privacy is rudely interfered with by young voyeurs. The youngsters make a loud laugh and sprint fast to a higher point where they loudly announce what they saw in the beautiful girls.

Thank goodness, croaking frogs have never been known to scare cattle from taking a drink and so the girls complete taking bath and embark on the journey home.

No sooner do the girls finish hanging the laundry on the fence than they begin smearing the mud hut that serves as the sleeping den for the big boys. The skills of Kaptuya of drawing flowers come in handy as Kipchumba was surely going to be red if his cottage was not well decorated. Shortly afterwards, the big boy demands from Jematia the kettleful of tea and the doughnuts he had ordered. From then on, the cottage is converted into some kind of discotheque. The girls and other youngsters are continually entertained by melodies like *Tangawusi* and *Mamou* of Franco's T.P.O.K. jazz, Prince Eyango's *you must calculer* and Issa Juma's *Jeniffer* among other hits. It is here that the girls teen-age curiosity is realized as they send Yano, the young boy to eavesdrop at the window and bring back the report. After undertaking the dangerous mission, Yano, the clever one, brings the message verbatim.

"Babe, you are my sunshine...violets are blue, roses are red, sugar is sweet my girl, but not as sweet as you.... nice chic, I'd like to be more acquainted with you; you know that I love you real and right, don't you? I cant be more honest ... I'll do anything for you... please do not think I am flattering you... it is only that I am being out right sincere... It is the best thing I can do at the moment.... I'll love you for always girl........."

The eavesdropping came to a sudden end when the sixth sense of Kipchumba told him perhaps a fool was observing his going to his knees. Since this was the lowest a man could go, he had to be sure there was no witness to this exhibition of weakness. How can a two hundred pound muscular stud go down on his knees for a woman?! As he opened the door, he saw Yano disappear into the home compound.

As the sun moved towards *cherongo,* Jematia got ready to go for milk. It was at that time that Kipchumba emerged from his den and escorted the young lady back to her home. After collecting his wooden Sanyo transistor and an umbrella, the teenager clad in baggy trousers, a round-necked pullover, moccasins, white socks and cap, together with the belle they set off.　A stone throw to the girl's home, the teenager met old-time pals: Bavon and Ngofo ascending from the lowlands. After seeing the sweetheart off, the young men began talks on many issues and episodes that ended minutes after one A.M. at Bavon's cottage.

Absolute Power

IN PURSUIT OF POWER

Flanked by elderly mothers and a couple of unknown drunkards holding high the candidate's portrait, the flamboyant skilled orator makes his entry to the town-centre from the direction of the post office. From this point, he can clearly see that a number of voters have assembled at *Kapkeyes,* the traditional venue for final election campaigns. A diehard supporter realizes that a quiet entry could undo the effect of grand campaigns that have hitherto been carried out and quickly, he leads the seventy plus supporters in chanting a rather moving lyric that goes:

Wendei ...wendei Chelang'a - Chelang'a will make it
Ee Legco .. olenjin okwe mapunjan ee koistogei... To legco
– Tell Maponjan to keep off
Wendei ...wendei Chelang'a - Chelang'a will make it
Ee Legco ... olenjin okwe mapunjan ee koistogei... *To legco – Tell Maponjan to keep off*

Indeed, the song brings all to an ecstatic mood as noted in Chelang'as' rhythmic juggling of his wooden staff decorated with a cockerel's head. After a little hulla-baloo Chelang'a takes a centre seat in the dais.

Hardly had he settled when loud singing was heard from the direction of the cathedral. So loud was the singing that one octogenerian remarked that it reminded him of the traditional circumcision songs of the pre-independence times when initiates sung in praise of village heroes and chastised cowards like one Chemeri from Saimo. As it was expected, Chamanbuch made his entry to the sound of thunderous applause from all and sundry. An omen to his eventual win was observed by the keen ones when Chamanbuch's comrade from Lawan took to the podium and led in singing Chamanbuch's signature tune that was now a household song. It was not easy to stop the people singing:

Iyoni ngo chichi?	*Who approves this aspirant?*
Iyoni	*He is approved*
Iyoni boisiek	*The old men approve*
Iyoni asak iyoni.	*He is wholly approved.*
Iyoni ngo kirgit?	*Who approves the bull?*
Iyoni	*He is approved*
Iyoni chitugul	*Everyone approves him*
Iyoni asak iyoni	*He is wholly approved*
Iyoni kole nee	*How is he approved?*
Iyoni kole wei iyoni asak iyoni.	*By acclamation: Yes he can!*

They sang and sang again.

No sooner had the song faded than the incumbent Laurien made his rather chaotic entry. Clearly, his supporters had taken the stuff from Meru in plenty and quite a number were still quite high on a drink definitely not from the East African Breweries. Still, the old time melody that went:

Kiyoku werikab soin	*The young men from the lowlands*
Barwe kole abirchin	*Have a single message*
Kura Silas Laurien.	*Vote for Silas Laurien*

Was enough to make everyone present feel the incumbents arrival.

Out of the blue, Mapunjan the rival candidate in his Land Rover short wheel base and lorryful of longtime supporters doning *Sinende* and other traditional paraphernalia arrived in the square. As he made an ascent to the platform, the wild looking allies repeatedly recited loudly:

Kenu, kenu lomin kenu	*The envious will have it rough*
Kilom iman lenjin bo	*You have envied – but we*
Kura mapunjan.	*Will vote for mapunjan.*

The chant went on and on and on.

Filled with a human population numbering not less than five thousand men and women, the sleek and princely motorcade of the kingly candidate hardly found a parking bay. The deviation from the singing game in itself was a style of its own kind. The mean looking bodyguards doning dark specs and dark suits reminded many of the old days when certain arrivals made the forefinger erect for a period close to an hour.

The time is two o'clock in the afternoon and speeches have to be quickly made to give candidates an opportunity to make another last minute 'meet the people' campaign on their way to their native land where

their umbilical cords were buried. Mapunjan, De-
mabior's look-alike gets the first opportunity to address
the multitude that shall decide his fate in twenty four
hours time.

"Great people of my motherland, I salute you in
the living spirit of the oracle of the hills and the caves.
My people, you all know my singular objective in this
race is to uplift the living standards of Arror both here
at home and those in diaspora.

I shall remain steadfast in poverty alleviation and
promise to perpetually lead the way in eradicating
ignorance by continually remitting a huge sum of my
honoraria to constituency bursary scheme. Ladies and
gentlemen, make a wise choice. Let's vote in dignity
and tranquility during this time of transition".

All the time Mapunjan was making his oxford
accented speech, the old women, illiterates and
drunkards were clicking loudly claiming that Mapunjan
was abusing them because they did not go to school.
Such pompous speeches made Mapunjan happy, as
inwardly he was proud of his academic feat. As others
complained, another group loudly cheered because they
knew the cheering would make them go home with huge
windfalls of cash when the sun sets. Mapunjan, as his
name suggested, was famous for giving out cash in
'wholesale' not in 'retail' like Laurien.

When the incumbent legislator took to the podium,
the whole lot of drunkards and intoxicated touts were
all smiles. As they laughed loudly, so did their
candidate.

"Voting for me is voting for development. I've been very good... I have given your children jobs, I am handsome. Vote for me, please. I have built very many maternities for your pregnant women.

Tomorrow morning who will you vote for?
Yesterday, one man brought many women to my house and told me they need my help. I asked... will I manage all these women? Who will you vote for tomorrow? The airie youth went wild applauding their man who was neatly dressed in a Nyerere suit, a godfather, shining shoes and armed with a beaded billy club.

Slowly, the oldest of all candidates left his chair and went to the centre of the dais. Everyone knew the guy was losing the race but somehow everyone liked him. It appeared he also was aware of the fate that awaited him but he seemed driven by an adage that said 'A bull dies with grass in his mouth.
"*Murenju bo Arror, mautye moso katwalenyi ak kile boisiek ta Ngenam tany chotin konget met...* (Gentlemen, old habits die hard and I only need a little push".

I know you all know that nobody can pluck out someone else's mushroom.   The whole crowd broke into loud laughter given the facial expression that suggested that he badly needed the parliamentary seat.

"My people, I once tried to get this seat from a Chumo. I clearly remember how I threw Chumo during the wrestling match but to my great surprise I found myself on the ground and Chumo squarely seated on my chest. After a hard search, I discovered that in his ankle was a chain tied to the ankle of the Samson in the hill. I backed off until Chumo handed the mantle to Sowe.

"Many times I said *baba*! And schools were constructed. I again said *baba*! And electricity was brought." At this point, people were dead with laughter.

"Arror, do not laugh at my saying *baba*! If ministers can say *baba*! … who am I not to? My people, if you want an educated man, please tell me so that I can tell Propesa vice chancellor of Nairobi University to give me even a degree in Bachelor of Arts. So ladies and gentlemen, please let me take this nubile bride."

As chemanbuch was taking to the podium, a helicopter of one of the absentee candidates came very close to landing. The Sowe man quickly remarked that the chopper was surely discarding the 'suitors' votes. Hours later, it was rumored that a number of cows including Sirwoi had aborted as a result of the loud noise made by the private chopper.

"My people, first receive greetings from the elephants at Kapnorok. They are fine" begun Chemanbuch when he finally took to the podium "I appreciate the support and hospitality you have accorded me during the numerous visits to your homes and neighbourhood … Thank you and be blessed. I need not overemphasise the fact that I shall not relent in my mission of ensuring that all homes from Agorayan in the east to Muchukwo in the west, Lelian in the south to Kinyach in the north be provided with piped water within 200 days of the life of the next parliament. Further …I guarantee you this day that upon my being elected as your servant in the august house, all monies otherwise known as the C.D.F shall be appropriately utilized and shall be accounted for to the last cent. It is an open secret that my commitment to education of our young people and securing employment for the youth has been my number one agenda. Before the almighty God, I swear now that I shall not rest until a working bursary scheme is established and until every location gets a decent primary school including the rehabilitation of our good school Bartolimo secondary school. It is important for us to ensure that come the formation of next government, people of Arror are in it...therefore, we should not stick to parties whose names read stench when read from the rear.

I guarantee you that mine is the winning party led by the great helmsman from the lake... that ultimate warrior who shall salvage this great nation from years of misrule characterized by acute cronism and tribal malignancy.

My people, vote the right person... be blessed. Thank you very much and I remain your person of yesterday, today and tomorrow"

The dark clouds that had been patient all the while finally gave in to torrents. How the people wished they had also heard speeches of the scribe who swears in bars by flapping his willy on the beer table.

As the crowd slowly melted in various directions one could not help remembering the many scenes and episodes that characterized the entire campaign period.

A story is told of the emergence of people who were thought to be long dead in mini-meetings in villages.

In one meeting at Tenyarnyar, characters resembling the early man and other inhabitants of Kamasia closed district before 1952 were seen in the public for the first time in twenty years. They are the 'Merochumba' as evidenced by their difficulty in recognizing a five hundred shilling note given out by Mapunjan.   Their knowledge of currency exists up to the coin of king George. One strange astigmatic Chelugo Maambosha was asked to comment on the campaigns but quickly shrugged his shoulders and asked the people to talk about the Dikdik which was clearing beans at Borkolu and Mal areas.

With the illuminations of the sky by the orange sun, comes memories of the pleasant and ugly moments of the campaigns. It goes without saying that the candidates' spouses had to bear difficult situations as certain people had literally abandoned their homes and perched at the Mheshimiwa's house because a meal was guaranteed there. The aspirant's personal life was brought to the fore through besmirching leaflets meant to assassinate the character of an opponent.

Children would of course live to remember the long caravan of campaign vehicles and the many posters pinned at the shopping centre and even in their schools. Others like Chesaina will quickly wish to forget the campaign times as they recuperate in hospitals following skirmishes and violence that emerged when 'Machine' tried to hide the tea beneath his Y- fronts. Were it not for Kimutyo, the village idiot, Machine would be richer by twenty thousand.

As the campaigns come to a close, the health workers in the dispensaries and hospitals should surely prepare to receive pneumonia patients following their spending long hours in the forests awaiting aspirants. One more thing is also certain, in about nine months time children shall be born in as far as Kuikui and Bartum who shall not be resembling anybody in their respective neighbourhood.

But in solidarity with their womenfolk, old mothers shall lie that the baby resembles one grandfather of Kipnyekew age set. The truth, the wise men say shall come to the surface in about thirty years when the "baby" shall begin to exhibit the powers of Shaka of the Zulu. Such are the times, Tom, Dick and Harry shall claim ownership and humanity will realize prostitution did not end in the times of Sodom and Gommora.

Many voters shall have difficulty making a choice when left alone in the voting booth as they shall be haunted by the promises they made to vote when they took the aspirant's money. Many shall vote for the highest bidder, while others shall choose to spoil the vote by voting for all the candidates, or practising their drawing skills on the ballot paper.

Absolute Power

AUGUST SUNDAY

Ngriii................ Ngriiii, the telephone rang at a rather ungodly hour. It was half past two in the morning. Dad woke up and tiptoed to the sitting room unaware that I too had heard the phone and was already on the extension.

Hello Sir!

Are you ready?" came the question
"yes,..................... *Ndiyo.* ....*Afande* .... I will ensure that everything goes on as planned by the Seven Ten Movement".

From behind the door, I realized Dad was not in his bluish Pyjamas but in full combat gear armed with a bazooka, a .45 colt and an HK-21 machine gun and was definitely not reporting for duty as he had done for the fourteen years he has been in the Armed forces. Soon Dad was gone.

Despite my age (I was eleven), I got an instinct to switch on the TAI radio transistor and tune to the only local station. The music I heard was neither hits like *Sandoka* and Co-operation (Odongo) of Luanzo Makiadi Franco and his T.P.O.K Jazz nor Miriam Makeba's *Hapo Zamani* as we were used to but rather some threatening lyrical and indeed quite unfamiliar melodies.

Occasionally, shots could be heard in the background and the orders of a rather illiterate drunk came to the fore.

Thirty five minutes later, a very familiar voice addressed the Murino Democratic Republic.

"I am Colonel Carlos Ramos, the protector of the sturdy youth and the leader of the Seven Ten revolutionary movement. I wish to inform you that beginning now I am the President of the Republic. All members of the public are instructed to remain indoors until further notice and the regular police are also ordered to surrender their guns to the nearest station."

Jesus Christ of Nazareth! That voice was definitely *Dad's*!. Everything that I had seen for the last one month quickly came to my mind. Those long silent meetings! Those journeys, the wry smile at the senior officers, the orders that I should never enter his bedroom lest something explodes. The voice confirmed my fears.

But this address did not last. Gun shots rent the air again and another authoritative voice which sounded like that of a man from the Northern Frontier District ordered the famous newscaster to inform the nation that His Majesty's government is still in control and that members of the Seven Ten Revolutionary movement have been vanquished. Alube's song "we are moving forward' was played a thousand times that day. It took thirty-six hours for me to hear of Dad again. The moment I saw him in hand cuffs, with his shackle attached to a massive shot-put and wearing a wretched face, I knew his days were numbered.

Malik, a close friend of Dad once came to our house and gave me fare to travel to our rural home. On my way home, I checked on Marquez to find out Dad's fate. His house had undergone a complete metamorphosis. The Sanyo music system, the Philips television, the Olympus camera and the Nigerian Agbala clothes were definitely not bought with salary. Many months later, I learnt that in the Pandemonium that followed the unrest, he had looted the electronic show room down town.

The lead police car and the jungle Land-Rover were now a common sight at our home. Anyone who was closely associated with Ramos was subjected to a rigorous interrogation. Many men went mute after being released from the mobile police station and women who had the misfortune of being interrogated, months later gave birth to babies who did not resemble anyone in the neighbourhood because of their light skin and short, curly hair.

Father Kibariki's visit to our home brought a smile on my face. In ten months, this was the only man I knew that I could associate with Riombo barracks for he was our Parish priest. His looks said it all. He was not an emissary of good news. After a lengthy one sided talk, I learnt dad had gone to the land of No Return. A court martial had sentenced him to death by lethal injection and his remains were lying somewhere unknown. The smuggled letter containing his will and the Oris Swiss watch remain the only mementos of that August Sunday.

Absolute Power

ABSOLUTE POWER

The six-foot tall, chivalrous hercules came to power in the tiny Caribbean country of Mendoza at a time when majority of the citizens were virtually fed up with the leadership of the aged president. The president, a maniacal strongman, bred a cult of personality by holding mass tribal ceremonies where dancers would perform spectacular routines, chanting his name for hours at a time while he watched from his throne typically wearing a *Kitenge* and open shoes.

For close to half a decade, the old president who adorned a goatee was not quite the chief, for all his powers had been "grabbed" by a certain clique of self-seekers who happened to hail from his neighbourhood. In a misleading effort to assure the public that he was still as fit as a fiddle and therefore able to lead, the president referred those in doubt to the first lady who could confirm the lion's prowess. Fotso, one member of the clique and a powerful minister in charge of internal security, was so drunk with power that he made any being who opposed the leader disappear. Rumors even circulated among the Hoi Polloi that Fotso slept in a separate room from his wife for fear that he might reveal highly classified state secrets during his dream-talks. This clique had finalized all arrangements that were certain to make one of their own ascent to power when the president sleeps and fails to wake up. They had tasted power and simply could not live outside it. Their words had been law for so long that handing over power to a person not from the house that fought for the hard-earned independence was simply unimaginable. The freedom struggle was so entrenched in the hearts and minds of "house members" that the leader had once compared it to grabbing some morsel from the mouth of a hungry marauding lion in the Masai Mara game reserve in East Africa.

The sad reality was that the president had ordered sadistic and gruesome tortures for his political opponents in order to crush and decimate any opposition. The aged and infirm men, women and children met the same fate. Mendoza women were tortured and were often raped and killed. Hundreds of them were placed in various rooms. Before their interrogation, they were disrobed, manhandled and harassed. During the grilling, they were burnt with cigarette butts and given electric shocks that were applied to their private parts, hands and mouths to extract a confession. Very often the victims simply committed suicide to escape their dismal fate. The cemeteries in Mendoza were in fact full of mutilated corpses.

Many of the detainees were blindfolded and beaten. Assassins and torture squads specially trained, professionally carried out their orders. A lot of the victims were men and women from the lake region. They were potential politicians, doctors, lawyers, teachers, professors and scientists.

In detention camps was a morbid stench that refused to abate. Detainees were served food once a day and that too had worms in it. Throughout the day and night, there emanated moans from people who suffered the bestial beatings they were forced to tolerate. The methods of torture were varied and unspeakable. The prisoners had their nails disgorged and were branded with electric burns on their bodies in sensitive places. Many people were blindfolded with their hands tied and beheaded and thrown into rivers. The practice was so rampant that the Mendozan Fishing Association had to stop work for several weeks as they found pieces of human flesh in the stomachs on the fish.

The spirit of death was known to take people's soul shortly after midnight. That was when the old leader died. His untimely death came at a time when most of the 'clique' members were on official duties abroad. It was therefore a big blow to them, for their plans to pour concentrated Sulphuric acid on the long serving vice president had been squashed by what others called the hand of God.

The approachable, down-to-earth new leader seemed to all to be their anointed leader like the Biblical David, son of Jesse. The countrymen had never known that a president smiled and that his entourage was normal persons. For the first time, the people saw a smiling president, a president who traveled on foot during his development inspection tours in the rural areas. Within a short while, His Magnificence had become so popular that the people started calling him the president for life. His popularity was partially a result of his ability to mix freely with the public but more so because of his unmatched generosity of helping the financially crippled with some handouts.

Five years since the demise of the founding leader, His Magnificence, Honorable Esperanza Zangi had sat squarely on the golden stool in the House on the Hill. The five years were enough for him to learn all the ways to live and act like a Caribbean ruler. So much of his present monstrous character had been a result of the way local leaders and citizens handled him. Cheated by the handouts, the people had come to compose songs perhaps compared only to those the supreme choir of Angels sang in praise of the Almighty Father high up in Heaven. From far and wide came songs that urged all and Sundry to salute our beloved president. The people from the Western and Eastern parts of Mendoza were notorious for these panegyric tunes. Their talented teachers in High schools and even in the public universities daily composed sweet melodies to appease the God given leader. Their lyrical and highly metaphorical tunes could as the coastal people would say eject the snake from its abode.

These melodies were played on the national radio and television channels so often that the people automatically learnt the songs by heart. Among the well-known tunes was one composed by a teacher from Western teaching in His Magnificence School with lyrics encouraging Zangi to keep on with his development projects in Mendoza while giving him the mandate to rule the Republic for life.

A regularly played campaign song had the following lines:

Mendoza people
Get out in the street
Run through all the zones

Shout as loud as thunder
To support the candidature of Zangi

Let us say it sincerely and frankly
Let us drop hypocrisy and ingratitude
Who better than Zangi
Can take care of our nation's destiny?

For all of us
Our only candidate is Zangi
You have been sent to us by God.

In the buses and cars
In the trains and planes
Our candidate is Zangi
For the patients in hospitals
Zangi is our candidate
Even if you are in prison for your mistakes
When you are out
Remember that our candidate is Zangi.

Workers in all the companies in Mendoza
Kilowatt, Mendoza Airlines, Unilever, Trade winds,
Mendcom, V. O.M. Sealand Express, Kulayote,
Railways, Tourist Board – Our candidate is Zangi.

Let us pray to God
Catholics, Muslims, Legio Marias,
Protestants, adherents of Musambwa,
Salvation Army, Traditionalists and Animists
Let us pray to God to give him long life
So he can stay at the head of our country Mendoza.

Others sang that the ceremonial wood, which critics saw as a lethal weapon, was actually leading the Nation to greater heights of development.

The hyperbolic speeches by the civic leaders and the parliamentarians made His Magnificence Zangi drunk with power. The leaders showered him with all manner of praise. They addressed him as the God fearing enlightened guide, benefector of the fatherland, saviour of the people, the father of the nation, Rebuilder of the financial independence of the republic and The Great helmsman. The chairman of the ruling political party even addressed him as the Prince of Peace, the Everlasting Father. The parliamentarians perpetually urged the Countrymen living in the plateaux, Mountains, hills and the lake regions to be absolutely loyal to the president and the political party, which builds the Nation.

Power corrupts; absolute power corrupts absolutely. This saying by a sage of the past cannot be more true especially given His Magnificence new manner of handling issues. His Magnificence's contempt for alternative thinking from the learned scholars at the university was made clear when he appointed nincompoops, illiterates to head parastatals and made them mouthpieces of his ideologies. They were so unlearned that one of them demanded that Mendoza have only "one political multiparty". A veteran freedom fighter sent as an emissary of peace to appease the striking university students even offered to buy 'this dialogue' the students demanded so that they could take home some doughnuts. The Kamuzu Banda lookalike from the president's constituency who was a permanent member of the entourage during the president's trips abroad once wondered loudly why this man from the Middle East causing fuel shortages shouldn't be expelled from the ruling party and asked the people to stop disturbing the president because all countries even the United States had their own Zangi. Such were the people who called the shots.

Sooner than later appointments for top government posts depended not on your credentials but on your Mother Tongue. His Magnificence appointed the Finance Ministry Chiefs from his backyard for reasons that you needn't be a professor in molecular immunology or nuclear physics to discern. The country's currency notes had signatures of people from one region. No wonder the country's monies were like tissue papers during the campaign period. The Heads of Internal Security were all from the president's hometown of Tadozo.

An awful sight came to the fore during the national day celebrations when the Father of the Nation was inspecting a guard of honour mounted by the armed forces. The troop commandant was Zanda, the chief of General staff was Zanchez, the aide-de-camp was Zamboka, the head of president's security escort was Zavi and the commander in chief was His Magnificence himself, Zangi Esperanza. Critics all over, including the stout reknown critics teaching literature at the public Universities were certain the conversation during the inspection of the guard of honour was not being conducted in the national language.

His Magnificence's power was real given the way people were expected to conduct themselves when expecting a visit by the Head of State. Schools were

ordered closed and it was mandatory that school
children and teachers line up along the rough roads
and sing and clap loudly as the president's fuel guzzling
Lexus, Daimlers, Jaguars, Prados, Range Rovers and
other State of the art limousines snaked by. It was law
that should the lead siren screaming presidents escort
car pass, then the travelers in public service vehicles
were to quickly alight and show the salute of the ruling
party as they shout on top their voices "long live Zangi!"
until the last escort car has long gone.

A clique similar to the one that surrounded the
former President started emerging, this time led by a
diminutive soft-spoken man from Zangi's village. So
powerful was he that he called himself software and
anytime he entered the august house, other
parliamentarians stood up in his honour. His
mushrooming riches were enough evidence of his total
access to where the money was stashed. Characters
who leveled accusations on him were soon converted
to the status of the living dead. He was particularly
notorious for asking the president to sack top civil
servants in a very odd manner. It was a known fact
that critical decisions concerning the state were made
when the president was traveling abroad. As soon as
Mendoza Air One stabilized at forty thousand feet above
sea level traveling at over eight hundred miles per hour,
the software and the president would issue terse
statements to the effect that so and so had been sacked
with immediate effect. The victim was always caught
unawares but keen observers had learnt that the
newscaster who adorned Afro hairstyle in the National
Television channel was more often synonymous to
shocking news from the powers that be. A chief
secretary who has since gone berserk had the

misfortune of being sacked with immediate effect at a time when he was delivering a talk on effective management to top civil servants and chief executives at a City hotel. His listeners vacated their seats when they learnt the news for he was now not the chief secretary anymore and his bodyguards and driver drove off the limousine to the nearest police station. Upon learning the news, the chief secretary made a desperate phone call to the House on the Hill to confirm but telephone numbers had long been changed and he found his call diverted to a butchery in one of the slums. The butcher politely asked him the quantity of meat he wanted.

Just to entrench his presence in the people's psyche, virtually every room had his potrait while institutions and facilities bore his name. There was Zangi stadium, Zangi Avenue, Zangi University, Zangi High school, Zangi international Airport, Zangi Hospital, Zangi Library, Zangi Dormitory, Zangi Teachers College. Name them. Zangi was Omniscient, Omnipresent and Omnipotent.

Absolute Power

AN EPISTLE OF THE DEPARTED

My dear brothers and sisters,

I know you are all in utter shock and seeing my body lying in state is something you have all failed to come to terms with. It was after a long deliberation that I decided to commit this abominable act. I could not stand it anymore and I just had to let my spirit go, and it is my hope that my incomprehensible action will one day set you, my dear brothers and sisters, free.

Jepkokwo, please stop sobbing. You are the eldest of us all and you are supposed to be condoling the young ones. I know you are very much annoyed with me and you wish I had shared any emotional turbulence that I have always had. Your mind should surely have recollected memories of our formative years when I was only two and you were seven. You would always bend and say to me 'Titi' and carry me on your back for that long distance to and from Turlenjun River. Do you remember the day people with a powersaw came to our neighbourhood to fell trees? It was our first time to hear such a loud noise and we thought the Rapture had taken place as our Sunday school teacher had always taught us. As usual, you said to me 'Titi' and you ran fast towards the bushes. It was on that day that you fell and your spinal cord was permanently damaged. All the time, our parents were taking alcoholic drinks at the *busaa* club and occasionally dancing to the tunes of *sarama*. Anytime I see you unable to walk, that painful memory is relieved. I hope my suicide will make other parents do their roles and stop letting children take care of other children.

I am certain Jemeli has heard the news and has rushed from her marital home. Now Jemeli, I would like you to kindly understand me. You know that we have shared a lot in life. The other day, I learnt you were unable to deliver through the natural birth canal. Were it not for the flying doctors from AMREF, you would now have become past tense. You were taken to the city hospital where the medics performed a caesarean section thus saving your life and that of my nephew, Barsongol. Jemeli, I want to let you know that that was as a result of the damage caused on your 'holy land' during the bizarre clitoridectomy. I know they literally scooped your genitalia and mended the vaginal tract to the size of a bean seed. The excruciating pain you felt made you faint for twelve hours. The pain was even more severe when passing water. An old woman had to insert a 'calabash pipe' on your urinary tract so as the urine does not come in contact with the wound. Now you know the bold step I have taken is a sign of the love I have for you and all other girls in the clan. My demise will make the torturers think twice before they subject another girl to this unnecessary mutilation.

I now want to turn to you Kimosop whom I know has refused to shed tears because that is a sign of weakness. You know what is important in life and what is irrelevant. Please, go and have a look at yourself at that large mirror in my room. Tell me, was it fair for the elders to subject you to all those rituals. You persevered some terrible pain when your six lower teeth were removed without an anesthesia using some crude Acheulian tools. As a result, you lay on a mat for a whole four months suffering from Tetanus. As if that was the tip of the iceberg, you later underwent weird tattooing ceremonies all in the name of becoming a man. Look at your shoulders and your arms. What is the purpose of those several scars? On your face are thousands of marks and your ears have hollow ear lobes. Your stomach is contoured and you are permanently armed with a spear standing on one leg like the Flamingo in Bogoria. Son of my mother, I wanted to fight these rituals and death was my only weapon.

At this moment, I know the twins (Jesire and Kipkorony) have still not come to terms with my unexpected journey to the land of no return. Jesire, you are now twenty-three and a cute nubile. Lovely sister, it makes me sick that your freedom to choose a spouse is non-existent. Long before you discovered you were a woman, our parents had sealed your fate. You were made destined to marry the bald headed sixty-year-old miser who is rumoured to be a sorcerer. I have shed tears many times on this. I want you to know that you deserve the best on this earth. You need a young, handsome man who will appreciate you beauty. Kipkorony, do you realize the right that our elders have denied you? Every morning, as the Children of the rich go to school, you sing tunes so that the cattle may follow you to the grazing plains. The elders are yet to identify a girl who can be your wife. You know as much as every young man knows that you will have to give twenty heads of cattle, forty sheep and ten camels as dowry for the chosen girl. Your marriage is pre-arranged. Are you contended with this? Many a time you have risked your life looking for these animals when you raided the Samburu in the North, Marakwet in the West and the Suk in the East. Who will benefit if you perish during this nonsense? If your senses are working you will appreciate my sacrifice. It was the only way I had to fight these archaic barbaric and obsolete practices.

Finally, my dear brothers and sisters, my executive decision was catapulted by events which touched my own person. You all know that when a man is of age, he is supposed to identify a site to build his house. Two months ago, I told the old man about my desire to put up a structure at Tuptup. I didn't know I had touched a rattlesnake. You should have seen his facial expression and the venom, which oozed from his mouth. In his annoyance, he ordered me to keep off from the fertile Tuptup and build at Yatianin, that Sahara in our village.

I end my missive by wishing you all the best in life. Let me hope we will meet on the Judgment Day which Josephina our Sunday School teacher often talked about. Pray that God, the Almighty father rests my soul in eternal peace. I wish you peace and hope that you will understand my unprecedented action.

Your brother,
Stephano Chumo

ETERNAL TWELVE HOURS

"Hey Kijana! It is long past eight and you are still in bed? Can you get out of bed and quickly make the necessary preparations. We should be in your new school by noon." Those were the terse words of Yusuf, the Army Sergeant-Major, to his son Musa who was due to report to form one in a city school.

Musa, of course, had not been a lazy boy. But it hadn't been his fault today to wake up long after sunrise. He had all along lived in the rural area of Modogashe and his mind had been conditioned to the cockcrow, that unfailing alarm which wakes the villagers by four thirty. But today, he was waking up in a house in the barracks near the city. Musa, hurriedly took a cold shower and by ten thirty he was doing a costly shopping with his father in one of the school uniform outfitters situated somewhere in a street named after a war veteran.

Shortly after the damn expensive shopping (Mr. Yusuf parted with a whole five thousand shillings which was a lot of money in the eighties), the journey to the High School began. Musa had to be led by the hand for he simply could not cross the busy Avenue. He was not to blame since in his home area, there was only one Motorcar, a Land Rover, which belonged to a merchant called Suleiman. It is the car he had always ran after in his childhood when it was ferrying merchandise to the lowlands. His mind had a quick flash to those days when he and other children dressed scantily waved continuously to the driver of the land Rover while chanting to their delight a best wishes tune.

They crossed the busy street and then walked past a beer depot and soon they were in the bus station situated near the big religious dome. Musa's father looked quickly at the buses and upon seeing a bus with a board labelled twenty-three, he grabbed Musa's luggage and informed him that that was the bus that would take them to the High School. The bus was driven past some skyscrapers and soon it was on a flat stretch. Musa craned through the window and on the right, he saw satellite dishes. His father nudged him and informed him that that was the famous broadcasting house. Soon, it was time to alight for they had reached the bus stop near the high school.

The time was eleven O'clock and the day was Tuesday the 24th of January. Musa, who was now neatly dressed in a light blue shirt, khaki shorts, navy blue pullover and grey stockings, walked steadily to the reception hall to await further instructions from the High School teachers. After a short while, his father was called to the bursar's office and a few minutes later, Musa was to accompany his father to the Principal's office. The tidily dressed gentleman donning spectacles welcomed him to the school that produced gentlemen. Mr. Yusuf then took a few steps back, clicked his heels, and gace a full military salute to the principal. After the formal reception, he went to a corner of the expansive pitch with his father to receive some valedictory pieces of advice. It was during that talk when Musa learnt of his new school having been once the institution reserved for the sons of the White colonial masters. Since Mr. Yusuf was expected to be on duty that afternoon, their conversation ended shortly afterwards.

Ding! Dong! Ding! Dong! rang a giant bell situated in a high tower and   from all corners boys emerged. Boys dressed like Musa were running helter-skelter while the big, well-clad gentlemen in long trousers and blazers were having a slow walk to their cubicles. One of the students in a differently colored necktie called Musa and showed him the direction to the junior dining hall. In his naivety, Musa ran across the out of bounds quadrangle. Upon arriving at the other end of the quadrangle near the dining hall, another student in a different tie (Musa later learnt that they were junior prefects) gave him several *ngotos* (painful punches on someone's head) and quickly ordered him to join other rabbles in the queue. Minutes later, a tall, serious looking young man gave the rabbles a signal that they should enter the Dining hall. Whilst inside, the "First Formers" kept on standing beside the dining tables awaiting the arrival of the tall man. His entrance was marked by total silence by everyone. He walked to a raised ground and hit a knocker like a high court judge and said a short grace which went:

> "Let us be truly thankful
> to God for what we are about to receive".

The villager in Musa soon came into the limelight. The meals on the table were totally alien to him. The rice, meat stew, fruit salad and bread pudding were meals Musa was seeing for the first time. His lunch had all his life been roasted maize and occasionally *githeri*. Hell began soon afterwards. Musa did not know how to use the provided fork, table knife and spoon and his instincts told him to just take the fruit salad directly from the bowl to his mouth. The head of table was not impressed and Musa was punished to kneel down in the dining hall until everyone else had left.

When the continuing students went to class for the afternoon lessons, Musa and the other new arrivals were kept in the waiting bay. It was then that Musa felt homesick like never before. Reminiscences of the rural life, his mother and young brother taking cattle to the stream, a flash back to the sight of his departing father made tears roll down Musa's cheeks. His was a total nostalgia for the days he was a celebrity in the village primary school. All of this, coupled with the fact that he was now a non-entity in this new environment, caused him a severe headache.

At four o'clock, the bell rang and the junior prefects came to pick Musa and his group. Nagila, a junior prefect helped Musa carry the metal box to Dorm four, compartment one of Tana House. There in, a parade was called and Musa, Lesasuyan, Washuma, Tsimba, Longomo, Ogulla, Ali, Ngorosishe, Magonya, Orwa, Kataka, Vadgama, Bird, Mureithi, Rorat, Metet, Isoe, Keriasek, and Abdul were given a list of the who's who in the school. The newcomers were to learn the list by heart and give the right answers when demanded. They learnt that the Principal was Kyungu, his deputy was Njoroge, House master was Mr. Kinuthia, Head of house was Gichuhi, senior house prefect was Anyanda, Dorm prefect was Salat and compartment Monitor was Nagila. The Advanced level prefects were so big that Musa answered the head of house was Mr. Gichuhi when asked who the head of the house was. He simply could not imagine him a student. The continued wrong responses by the new comers made them be quickly subjected to the accepted mode of punishment in the institution. The rabbles were ordered to get in to games kit and then the tedious physical exercise began. Long'omo the boy from Lokichar led in counting thirty press-ups, Rorat counted the twenty stand-jumps. Musa counted thirty frog-jumps. Then, the punishment came to a temporary halt for questioning again. A second round of wrong responses, irked Nagila badly and the rabbles were ordered to go behind the house for further "torture." On the way out via compartment two, a new comer, Kunyobo was crying loudly lamenting why his father brought him to this hell of a school. Swao, the chaos, the compartment monitor was continuously giving him hard knocks.

Musa led in counting the thirty sit-ups on the sloppy ground. Kataka counted a hundred 'beckons' with hands in the air. Different liquids have different boiling points and so do men have different breaking points. It was in count number seventy that Ali from Wajir and Bird, the Kenyan of European ancestry fainted. The physical torture came to a halt but the punishment was to continue in form of manual work. Isoe was to weed flowers, Orwa to mop the dormitory, Rorat to remove cobwebs, Ogulla to spread the bedding while Metet and Musa were to clean the toilets. The punishment was to be completed in ten minutes.

Close to supper time, everyone was expected to shower, tidy up and report for inspection. Mujera, the other fourth form prefect did a thorough inspection of the rabbles shirt collars, shaven heads, stretched stockings and ironed shorts. Those who were not tidy to the prefect's standards suffered further punishment. In the dining hall during supper, Musa had difficulty using fork and knife but this time he was lucky to receive tutorials from S.R Obbayi, another form one who had reported a week earlier. Taking meals was such an orderly event that all students were supposed to finish eating at the same time. Quick swallowing of food was considered a characteristic of those who are atavistic; comparing well with the early man

Supper ended at 6.40 p.m. and there was still a short time to prepare for evening preps, but Musa was to find it another rough moment. Ogolla, a notorious third former called him to buy a combination (samosa and Chapati]. Once Ogolla was through, he instructed Musa to go to a nearby tree and do to it everything that is done to a girl. Musa had to undergo the embarrassment of hugging the tree and telling it words like "You are my sunshine, I'll not even love you for ever because to me forever is a shorter time!" Ogolla, the bully did not stop there.

After, giving Musa the definition of a "rabble", as a form one was called in those says, Ogolla gave him another serious *ngoto*. He defined a rabble as a character, in fact, a domesticated gibbon with all the characteristics of the early man, to be specific, an equivalent of *Astrolopithecus Boisei*.

The preps bell rang and Musa went to get his books from the dorm and quickly rushed to the tuition block. He was already late for preps. After squatting for a few minutes, he was ordered by a roaming prefect on duty to write five hundred lines saying "I will never be late for preps again" and a full copy of the school rules.

That was to be done within the time allocated for preps. Meanwhile, a gang of form threes had taken over the first form tuition block ready to molest the rabbles. Had it not been for the God sent, coming of the Head of school, G.Z.O Nyotumba, the rabbles would have been inflicted with a very painful experience. After handing in the school rules and the five hundred lines, Musa packed his books but Alas! A copy of *Physics for today and tomorrow* and an expensive copy of *Chemistry: Complete course* were missing. In his dazed mind, the otherwise three minute walk from the tuition block past the physics labs to Tana, the house of terror, took Musa a whole fifteen minutes.

Musa, to this day is said to have fresh memory of the first twelve hours in the city school: his uttermost terror.

Absolute Power

THE LANDING

The sun-rays penetrate through the enigmatic hill of Nuregoi which stands above the plains of Kaptiony. Against this backdrop, the little village of Sanjun enjoys the beauty of the late afternoon sunlight and the natives find the sunshine conducive to attend to daily chores, like young girls collecting firewood from the nearby bushes, women threshing millet and the under-eighteen boys finding great pleasure in tending goats in the areas around Kew, the salt lick.

Kimala, a fourteen-year-old lad stood on a rock situated in front of his mother's hut gazing up at the wedge like formation of the crows fying in the sky above him. Their noisy caws broke the immense silence that lay like a blanket spread from the mountains of Borbora and Kukwarel in the south to the plains of Kasotwan in the North. Kimala turned slowly, watching the birds disappear to the south, thinking how Cheptumo his younger brother would have liked seeing them. He would have made up something about them like saying that the Pokot had sent the crows to spy on the Marakwet in preparation for a raid. Knowledge of birds migrating to breed was far beyond the villagers' comprehension as Kimala was after all the highest educated person in the plains with education of class two learning at the far Kapkiamo District Education Board whose only teacher was the class four graduate from the mission Inter - mediate school, Mwalimu Sowe.

Gome! Gome! Gome! Came the sound of *Tutung*, the drum, accompanied by the cry of a man from the far village of Lawan. The beating of the seldom used *Tutung* meant that the villagers had spotted something unusual. The words of a woman could be faintly heard and Kobilo, Kimala's mother and other women understood that locusts had been spotted at the farther plains of Kuikui.

"Kapluk eeh Kapluk" shouted a man announcing that the locusts had taken a turn towards Kapluk in the West hopefully saving Sanjun an imminent disaster of incalculable magnitude. But that was not to be. The locusts somehow miraculously took a U-turn after spotting the green veld of sorghum and millet in the upper village of Loten which wasn't far from Sanjun.

"Kiwechgei wee bich Kiwechgei." These words from a woman in Loten announcing that the locusts were seemingly landing sent a chill down the spines of the people of Sanjun.

The time was about three thirty in the afternoon but Chelanga, the drunk, thought it was midnight when he was awoken by Chemelil, his eldest son. Anybody else would have thought so because the billions of locusts had formed a dark cloud in the sky above Sanjun causing an eclipse of its own kind. The sound of the locusts' wings was terror to the young ones like Chebet and Kiptallam who clung to their mothers' tattered goatskins-skirts. The ghostly locusts landed and the villagers knew that their hard work would in a short while be rendered useless. In a bid to save what could be saved, the old men went to the middle of their millet farms and beat the loudest any object available, the oonly objects available were cow hides. Their efforts were in vain for they soon took cover in the bushes when thousands of locusts landed on them. Kiptui, was to joke weeks later that he took cover when he realized that some locusts had found their way to his 'balls' and the excruciating pain he felt made him think that one of the 'balls' was already down.

It took less than ten minutes for the green vegetation to vanish and the brown earth was exposed as though it was ready for ploughing. Heaps of locust-droppings left by the departing insects was the only benefit accrued from the invasion, for the land would definitely be more fertile come the next planting season.

Disasters come in torrents so goes an old adage. This could not be more true for as soon as the locusts took off, came the landing of a perfect predator. Flicking his wings lightly, the martial eagle descends on a nearby *Boyotwo* tree and scans carefully to see anything edible. Soon, it realizes that the Hares and other rodents have long taken cover. A slow turn of the neck coupled with a little bend, brings the sight of the fifty-pound infamous predator to a crawling creature at Kimala's home. The glide begins, the blurred wings spreading out in the air and the powerful legs eject like those of Boeing 747 preparing to land. Within a twinkle of an eye, young

Kimetto has been grabbed and his ascending cries bring the villagers to the horrific sight. The fanatically tireless flight of the eagle is like a wind of mortality but it seems to lack purpose. It is merely a pondering of possible prey, a contemplation of killing.

As the villagers watched in shock, the ghost that was now contouring the sunlit hillside with smooth unwavering flight, another spectacular event was taking place a short distance away. A fourteen foot black mamba lay flaccidly across the dark high igneous rocks of Chepatono looking a little dazed by the sunlight after the darkness that existed a short moment hitherto. In a moment, its tongue started to flicker in and out and it turned its head from side to side in an interested manner. Then with smooth fluidity it started to slitter through the rocks towards the burrow below. Slowly it drew closer and closer and when it reached the brim of the burrow, it peered down at the helpless hyrax caught between a rock and a hard surface, with its fierce silvery eyes. Its tongue flicked again as if it was smelling the rodent and it nosed it gently like a dog with a piece of sausages. It opened its mouth and started to engulf the hyrax. A mamba has a jaw constructed in such a way that it can swallow a prey that at first looks too big to pass through its mouth. The mamba neatly unfolded his jaws and the skin of its throat and soon the hyrax was disappearing in the Mamba's mouth. When the meal was an inch down his body, he paused to meditate and glided from the burrow up to its abode, a cave in a tree trunk.

News about the locust invasion came to the limelight again sometime around Christmas of that year. Chelimo , a foreman in one of the farms in the white highlands who hailed from the village narrated to the villagers how the locusts were petrol-bombed after they caused a massive destruction at *Kap Tangalass* farm near *Sisibo* in Uasin Gishu. The loss suffered and the terrifying events witnessed remain fresh in the minds of those who had the misfortune of witnessing the September, Nineteen Fifty Six locust invasion at Kilae Kugkit location in Kamasia District.

Glossary
Boyotwo – Baobab tree
Kap Tangalass – Doughlas' Farm
Sisibo – Sixty Four, present day Eldoret.

Absolute Power

A SATURDAY OF SOTS

It is 5.00a.m. on Saturday. The sun is still shy. In the distant bushes, the quails scatter noisily from the attacking wildcat, but Saina is already at work. His long beard, unkempt hair and the heavy sideburns give him the looks of a man in his fifties. But the village idiot is only thirty. Reliable information has it that the last time he took a bath was the day he was born and this cannot be more evident than the calloused heels that peer from his tyre sandals (*Kenyera*) which are obviously part of his sleeping rear.

Saina is up early because a man must drink. Tea is not part of his diet. Alcohol is what he consumes in large quantities and that is exactly why he is there at the wee hours. Like everyone else who has been hit by the high cost of living, Saina has learnt new ways of bringing his drink to the table. Today he has to fetch drums and drums of water from the distant stream, sieve and serve the brew to 'moneyed' customers so that he can get a precious swallow as the brew owner does the cashier's work.

Saina finds this a better option compared to those situations when he has to plough a fifteen by fifteen piece of land to get only three *Kapkawa's* of cream.

Besides, that kind of heavy duty requires company of other comrades who will provide rhythms that accompany the movement of the *Jembe*. But today Kipyegomen and others won't be there, for they are with the village son who works in a big company in the city of Nairobi.

Eight thirty finds the compound deserted. The brew is over but Saina is not even a quarter high after taking only two and half *Kimbos* of *busaa*. He looks at his childhood friend, Chongwo and somehow the message is communicated. They must go look for more brew. The journey begins towards West. Forty minutes later, they arrive at a known joint but sadly, the last drink is being served to an old lady. *"Chamgei Chorwe"* he greets the grandma as he and buddy turn direction to the South. A journey of three and half kilometres is nothing when a man badly wants a drink. The men arrive with sweat irrigating their dark backs and once again the liquid has all been consumed.

Eastwards they turn and embark on a thirty five minutes journey to the last known resort. After a sobering walk, they arrive at the den and to their greatest joy, there is liquor. Saina asks for a litre of the 'swallow'. He knows he will pay for it by way of cleaning the brewing apparatus.

Solemnly, he gets hold of the container full of the stuff and with tearful eyes he addresses the milky substance. "My precious drink, I will not even chew you but simply swallow you". In his view, chewing the brew was likely to cause it some pain. Halfway through, he looks at the drink and publicly declares that the drink is sweet but money is the problem.

Two in the afternoon finds them on the way to the nearest trading centre. Minutes, later they arrive at Tuheshimiane Club. Of course they have got no money but they are full of hope that another carousing comrade will buy them beer. And sure enough, Ricardo the guy they shared the knife with, arrives in style. Saina breathes a big sigh and cheerfully ushers the dear friend to the high stool while lesser mortals himself or his friend, take a lower seat.

Ricardo orders himself some dry gin and offers his pals some hotter whisky. Drinks have a way of slowly making someone become his real self. As the volume of the gin lowers so does the metamorphosis of Ricardo evolve towards completion. He begins to justify his taking alcohol. First, he mumbles that the bible says somewhere in book of Timothy that a little drink is good for a man. Then, he confidently announces that his gin is an aphrodiasic better than the concoction of rhinoceros horn and the alligators dry skin, and lastly declares that it is the only way he can have good times with buddies with whom he has shared wild and weird adventures.

It is four o'clock now, and the drink has climbed the higher zones of Ricardo's and Saina's minds. Saina dozes in the wooden bench. The liquor misleads Ricardo to think that he was once in Oxford and that he himself is a mobile dictionary. He unintelligibly constructs haphazard sentences with the words incognito, lugubrious, nincompoop,

vendetta, aficionado, syllogism, abracadabra and so
forth. He announces that he is not a small man as
many folks think but that he is well connected and
enjoys acquaintance with the world's Greats.
Olympic gold Medalists and the Who's Who in the
academic circles. He highlights his mental prowess
to the effect that he has learnt to the highest levels
Science like molecular immunology, nuclear physics
and space Science.

A slow turn of the head gives him a glimpse of
Rhoda, the gold digger whom he buys a drink after a
tight squeeze of her bottoms. His gaze at blonde's
rear is interrupted by the hawker's presence. The
vendor whom he had previously ordered to disappear
from his sight is summoned and is told of how his
merchandise is good. He quickly parts with money
thrice the actual worth of the cowboy hat that Ricardo
now places on his head. The merchant whose
patience is legendary like that of the vulture in Mara
plains smiles all the way to his ghetto.

Exactly eight is the time the butcher-man
informs Ricardo that his well- spiced beef fry is ready.
From a far part of his brain, a message is received
by Ricardo that his lovely wife Sandra and children
in the distant land of Urel are languishing constantly
feeding on edible weeds, some fungi, rarely offal and
wild berries to supplement their fruit diet. The
penultimate bottle takes Ricardo on a journey to the
distant past. With deep nostalgia accompanied by
genuine sobs, he reminiscences episodes and
remembers many friends who have gone to the Land
of No Return. His sombre mood is luckily cut short
when the bar man plays the melodies of Jean Bosco,

Orchestra marquis and of course Franco's Makiadi's *Tres impoli* and *Mamou.*

Ten in the night finds Ricardo about the only patron still on his feet. He searches for some cash but to his dismay two thousand is over. He swallows the last bitter sweet waters of Jeremia. In his frustrations, he sings loudly circumcision songs which border on extreme vulgarity. It is then that, Saina lazily wakes from his slumber. The guy begs to be given the hot stuff literary called *machozi ya simba* (the tears of a lion). The stuff is so hot that the man literally closes his eyes as he takes the half glass of the lion's tears. As the juice finds its way to wherever, the seller promptly ties the customer's ankles because sooner than later a man's bowels will be emptied clean. Ricardo and Saina slowly exit the beer hall and wobble in the wrong direction. Fifty yards away, they fall and black out.

Absolute Power

SEED OF EVIL

Onesmus Matende had somehow survived the violence these three weeks, partly because he had remained indoors most of the time and partly because no one was sure of his tribe. For all his 65 years of life, he had lived among the people of the lake in the city slums. After all, this is where his grandfathers were settled after they completed constructing the railway. On this chilly morning of 22nd January 2008, when he was frog-marched by the tobacco sniffing militia, the old man was not really sure of what was going to happen to him.

He was put together with other frightened "aliens". He heard their whispers and learnt that the militia had descended on the slum to revenge killings happening elsewhere. Interestingly, the ambush happened right when the law enforcers were looking on. Were they abetting? Or was it orders from above? Poor Matende sighed heavily "I just cast my vote and went home. Why didn't the man responsible just announce the true results?"

Tick- tock – tick – tock the clock chimed at mid day. All around Matende heard women screaming in a last effort to avert rape, men cursing using the strongest words possible and the terrified cry of children, as the militia shouted and pushed them here and there.

What do they want with children? Matende asked the person next to him. "Don't you see? The other answered, the children will be held hostage and tortured to make the opponent people's leader surrender his quest for the top seat. At the imagination of an innocent toddler weeping, uncontrollable sobs rolled down Matende's cheeks.

A young 'militia' man who somehow looked smarter than the rest was attracted by the sobbing. Slowly, he came and whisked the old man away to a tent a distant away serving as the militia's headquarters. The old man was frisked thoroughly and as he moved towards the table, he felt his knees weaken and throat swollen in anger.He was pushed further afield and after a while he was dragged before a parade of the militia. They gazed at him and decided to play with his mind.

"What is your name, *Kijana*? One of them asked him.
"Me? But he called me a young man". The laughter sickened him.
"Yes , you What is your damn name?
"Onesmus Matende"
"Where is your house from here?
"Near the bridge, off the railway"

The 'militia' Chief became alert and then roared, "Matende is a Tharaka name, right? Why do you side with them?"

The old man became confused. The Chief was reading a document with information about an old man living near the bridge. His suspicion that it was him was high. "Who do you live with? And please do not lie because if you lie to me your smooth face will never be the same again."

"I live in my ghetto," the tired old man mumbled. If only these militia would leave him alone. "You said you lived alone but from our informed and reliable source, you live with some three young men." The old man hesitated. For many years he had lived alone because the rest of his family resided in the rural area but for the last three days, he had been with Ochieng's boys. The Ochiengs had been his friends. When the violence escalated, the boys had been send to him for safety. That was as it should have been. What were friends for anyway?

After, bearing a brief torture, the old one spoke. "The Ochieng boys came to me after their father was shot at close range as he ran away from the uniformed officers". "Luos! So you housed Luos!" The militia men asked in unison. How unbelievable! The militia looked at him questioningly at his eyes. "Mr. Ochieng, the boy's father, was my friend. We have lived together as happy neighbours for many years. I was more than ready to give refuge to his sons."

"So you were a happy man- eeh? Didn't you feel you were betraying us giving refuge to sons of the enemy tribe"

"No. I did not and I do not"

"You should surely be ashamed. You are a member of the old association. You have a duty of protecting the leadership from slipping away. You are a mountaineer, not a canoeist. How could you protect them? You must be ashamed."

"No, I am not. I am only happy I offered them refuge."

"You have been in the government, my brother, and you know how sweet it is to be in power. You must do everything possible to guard the throne. Can't you see that all our sons and daughters have secured employment because we dominate the top positions in the civil service and Parastatals."

"I may have voted for the government side. Yes, that may so, but if being in government means I hate those not in, then I would rather not be part of the government. The Luos are the same as we are. What is wrong with being Luo?"

"They are Kihii's"

"I don't see Kihiism when I go to the hospital to be treated by the Neurosurgeon from the lake region neither do I realise Kihiism when the brilliant Professor articulates his party's manifesto during the TV Live debates. They are simply no different from us".

"Beastly kihii lover" a militia-man screamed as he gave the old man one karate kick on his rib-cage which could render a horse paralysed.

From his left pocket, the old man removed a carving knife and with all his might drove it deep into the militia chief's chest. The two men stared at each other as they dropped dead in opposite directions.

KIDNAPPED

The schools had been closed all over the country for Christmas holidays. Many students were loitering in the town chatting and bickering.

Occasionally, you could see students coming out and going into the national library. That early morning, I had been sent to the town by my mother to go and collect some items in the supermarket. The streets were busy, so I decided to walk on the pavement.

Screech! The driver slammed his foot on the brakes, a brand new black BMW stopped a few metres away almost hitting me on my butt. I could not see who was inside the vehicle since it was heavily tinted. But I was angry. Very angry. The idiot almost ran over me. He was going to get a piece of my mind, I made directly for the driver's side to confront him or her. But my anger immediately turned to horror, then a mixture of contempt and respect, when I found myself starring into the barrel of a gun!

Contrary to my expectations, the hand holding the gun belonged to a woman. She must have been in her mid thirties. She hid her eyes behind the dark sun glasses smiling. My eyes quickly took in the scene and I realised that the car had three other occupants, all of whom were men, dressed in expensive suits and wearing an expensive cologne. They looked like triplets waiting to exchange marriage vows with their brides. On my side, I was rooted on the ground by the power and fear of the gun.

The woman made a gesture to the two men in the back seat and before I knew it, I found myself sandwitched between the two perfumed men. I could also smell the oil shinning on their heads. They all looked serious, by their frowned faces. The engine roared back into life and the BMW slithered away leaving behind a black cloud of exhaust fumes. They all rode in silence for about ten minutes until I gathered enough courage to blurt out,   "Where do you think you are taking me? Wait till my dad finds you. He will strangle you to death." I regretted my outbursts almost immediately. The driver fished out a reefer from her brown handbag and lit it, drew a long puff, and turned round, blew the smoke directly to my small, oval baby face. Then her companion slapped me hard in the face. He hit me again and again and I began to cry loudly in pain.

Tears trickled freely down my cheeks, and she could feel them rolling down. For the first time the woman spoke. "Be a good boy and you 'll be okay. Just shut your mouth". There was finality on the way the woman spoke. Judging from the tone of her voice, I could tell that she was not the kind of a woman to be joked with. She was not like the women at St. Augustine academy with whom you could play and joke with. There was deadly silence in the vehicle. Deep down my heart, I could tell that there was something wrong going on. I was terrified.

The woman pulled out her handbag and removed another two reefers. She lit them and puffed all at once. I was petrified. The other three men did not care nor bother about her actions. They were conversing in Tamil, Uzbek or Gujarati. I could not understand. But I could judge by myself that I had heard that language on the T.V. I could only decipher that they were hired gangsters.

All this while, the woman kept throwing glances on the road and then on me. None of them noticed that bend on the road until they were almost there. The man in the passenger seat yelled out on top of his voice, "Britney look out!" A look of horror came across the driver's face as she contemplated negotiating the sharp turn. She slammed on the brakes and fought hard to keep the car on the road, turning the wheels this way and that way. But the car got out of the road and rolled several times before landing on a ditch. Only groans of pain could be heard.

As fate would have it, I survived the accident, with minor injuries. Britney also survived. The other three men died instantly having sustained deep cuts from broken pieces of glass. I thanked the living God for his merciful deeds. Britney couldn't find her gun. She unbuttoned the jacket of the dead man seated next to her and took out his pistol.When she turned to look at the men on the back seat, I wasn't there. Britney flung the door when she spotted

me on the highway. She aimed the gun at me and
fired two shots.   The first one went right into my leg
and the second went right through the chest of a
policeman who had just stepped out of his car to find
out what was happening.   When Britney reached
where the policeman lay dead in a pool of blood, I too
was lying on the ground groaning in pain from the
bullet wound. That moment her faced changed.

I knew she would murder me. Her eyes were
red like burning furnace. She then pointed at me
with her fore fingers, "You little brat, today is your
end!".   Her words pierced my heart like a knife.
Due to the lose of much blood from the bullet shot, I
fell unconscious. But when after a long while, I
regained consciousness, I found myself in a
comfortable chair. I was trapped on the seat by a
broad belt on my waist that made me uneasy.

There were several rows of similar chairs and
the structure of the room was strange. It had small
windows. I opened my eyes wider and rubbed them
to make sure that I was not having my usual
hallucinations. I couldn't believe it. It was real.
The structure I was inside was an aeroplane. I threw
a glance at the passenger seat next to Britney and I
could feel her hot tempers. She smiled back at me
making me even angrier than before.

Oh yes! I remembered it all. I tried to lift up my
leg but failed. The bullet inside had been removed
and it was heavily bandaged. I couldn't tell how
Britney had managed toi slip through the "tight"
Kenyan Security at the Airport. "Try anything stupid

and you'll be a corpse before I'm arrested, understood?" Britney shouted angrily.

I cooled down and started thinking hard what I had done to deserve all this. Religion is the only key which explains certain mysteries but it couldn't work at the moment. I was really confused. "Dear Lord, what have I done to deserve all this? Please help me to come out of this strange happening" I said in a silent prayer.After a short while, there was an announcement reminding passengers to fasten their seat belts before the aeroplane landed in Bahamas state Airport. The plane taxied down to the terminal and the passengers came out of the plane quietly minding their P's and Q'S. Britney made me sit on the wheel chair and pushed me inside a taxi. The area was too strange for me because I had never set foot on the American soil. The buildings there were taller than ours in Nairobi. The taxi sped to a beautiful house.

Although the house was small, I must confess that it was comfortable. I was fascinated by the living room. It was so luxurious that I forgot my suffering. There was a 54-inch plasma T.V.-set on the wall. A million shilling worth leather sofa set, stood on a flower carpet and three large tables with glass tops added to the beauty. Three guards were left to watch over me and with instructions to kill me if I proved uncooperative. They all kept watching me with red eyes. They were all serious and from my own observation on them I could tell that Britney paid them well for their work.

I relaxed and decided to watch the television. As soon as I switched on the television, the breaking news on CNN caught my attention "News reports from Kenya say that an American gangster is being hunted by the Kenya police force after she shot a policeman dead. Sources close to vigilance house said that Britney was earlier involved in a fatal accident that left three of her comrades dead. The bodies of the deceased are lying in the city mortuary. Meanwhile, the police are investigating the proximate cause of the bloody accident, which Britney survived. She apparently fooled the Kenya Airport security. She was accompanied by a boy of about seventeen years."

"Bastard! You daughter of a bitch. How dare you kidnap me and pretend that you are my sister. I wish I knew the cause of all this," I said as tears rolled down my cheeks. The guards never bothered with me but they kept on laughing sarcastically. The pain ran throughout my body and left me paralysed. I switched off the T.V. All of a sudden one guard slapped me on my temple forcing me to lie down. I lay down because I feared to be killed. Then he whipped me several times which made me sprawl on the floor.

I was tied with ropes on the chair and I had no alternative but to endure the suffering. By that time, I was very much discouraged about life and I wished the earth would open up its mouth and swallow me alive. But it did not happen.

Gong! Gong! There was a gentle knock at the door. The guard opened it without hesitation. A woman came in. "What's wrong, Jimmy, don't you recognize me?" She asked. I took a closer look on her and I realised that she had removed the sun glasses. "Of course, I recognize you," I muttered after a deep look. "Britney, yes Britney. How did you know my name?" She asked surprisingly. " And how did you know mine," I asked her.

She ordered the guards to untie me. I sat down on the sofa feeling uneasy, and eager to hear what Britney would say. "Jimmy, your loving daddy told me that he had a son by your name long time ago when we were students at Boston University. He was my classmate and we fell in love. But he betrayed me by going off with one of my best friends-Sandra, that's your mother. I know you don't understand all this but I must revenge whether he likes it or not.

"Don't worry your father will be arriving here tomorrow very early in the morning. His failure to show up will cost you your life. Keep these words fresh in the back of your mind......... I'm sure he values your life." She said and went away gesturing to the guards. She slammed the door behind her with a big thud! At that moment, I was shaking terribly.

Shortly afterwards, a beautiful young lady opened the door widely and she was carrying a roll of bandages. "My mum told me to help you change your bandages," the girl stammered. I must confess this. The girl was a rare type. She was very beautiful. Enchanting like a moon in a cloudless sky, her chocolate brown eyes glowed. She had sensual lips that parted to reveal a set of pearly, dazzling teeth and a voice which was soft and cool. She had long wavy black hair. Her firm shy breasts stuck out rigidly against her white cotton blouse, showing the outline of her nipples. Her eyes could barely keep on the task she was performing. Her beauty was bewitching.

"I'm Talia and you are...?", "Jimmy," I replied back". So Britney is your mummy? "Oh yes!, she said looking shy." I asked her with fear, "Who is your father" she replied saying that she had never known or seen her father all her life. "Mum says, my father lives somewhere in Kenya. Anyway never mind about all these, I 'll see him one of these fine days", she said tying the last bandage on my leg. What Talia had said made me cry. Now I knew she was my blood sister.

To our surprise, the door flung open and in came my dad accompanied by Britney. My daddy had arrived earlier than I expected. Tears were rolling down my father's cheeks. He came and embraced me crying, a father feeling the pain of his son. He kissed me on my cheeks to show his love and affection. He then turned back to Britney to find out that she was aiming the revolver at him. I screamed on top of my voice as she cocked the gun.

"Mr. Benson, you were my fiancé in the gone days, and you betrayed me by going with one of my best friends. Why did you do all that to me......why? you promised to marry me when you impregnated me and now I have your daughter Talia who has been fatherless. You'll have to die!"

The sound of a gunshot rent the air and Britney dropped on the floor badly injured. It was the FBI. They had arranged to arrest her since my dad gave them the all information when he wanted to board the plane. Talia ran to her injured mother. She wept as the police carried her to a waiting ambulance.

Talia was happy too see her dad for the first time in her lifetime. The next day we flew to Kenya and arrived home safely. I thanked God for saving my dad's life and mine too as I reminiscenced what we went through. Talia's mother has since been released from a correctional facility.

Absolute Power

A GLIMPSE OF THE DEITY

This story is about Tito, not his friends or his family, just about Tito. I know what is going through your mind right now, you are asking what is there of importance that I can say about Tito. And I will tell you Tito saw God! Impossible? Wait and see and then tell me what you think at the end of the story. Of course I'll start from the beginning, from the time Tito came into our village one fine morning with his baggage strapped to his back. There wasn't much but it was noticeable especially because of how dirty it all looked. He burst in with such zeal that not long after, everyone knew him and in their own ways, liked him. We did not know where he came from and cared less.

He did odd jobs for people in the village and earned his money in this way. He never refused to do anything and even the women sometimes left their babies in his care whenever they needed to rush to the market to buy their groceries. The only problem with him was that he drank too much. At first it was just a little *busaa* but it soon became *chang'aa* and then there was no turning back for him. This was when his problems began. He no longer got the odd jobs that the villagers used to give him and the women chased him away whenever he moved near their children. And so he grew dirtier and dirtier and sometimes even violent. He hardly had any food to eat unless a kindhearted person gave him some left-overs. I know what you are asking now; how did he get his *chang'aa*? Easy! He would sit outside the chang'aa dens and act as the watchman for them. It was illegal even then to brew this stuff and the police were always on the lookout for the culprits, but Tito outdid them. He would whistle if he saw the police coming and the brew would be cleared as everyone ran to safety. This earned him his daily dose.

Within no time he was just too dirty to sit near people and he moved to stay in the outskirts of the village. No one came to visit but it did not matter to him as long as he was allowed to go on looking out for the Police and getting his *chang'aa*. And it was when he was sitting under the old *soke* tree, oh yes, that very same tree. It hadn't yet been cut down by the greedy Kibet, but that's a story for another day. So as I had said earlier, he was sitting under this tree when he heard someone announcing that this Sunday was the day to watch as the Man of God would perform miracles at the crusade. Mmmmhhh.... A Man of God would perform miracles! It wouldn't hurt to go and see. After all, he had never seen miracles being performed and instead of sitting alone in his house nursing a terrible hangover, he would go watch this Man of God performing at his best.

And Sunday came and Tito perched himself on one of the trees far off from the rest of the congregation and waited for the miracles to begin. He did not care about the singing and the praising and the testimonies even from his very own customers! This did not matter to him as he waited only for the miracles. And then the Man of God came to the makeshift pulpit amid shouts of hallelujah and drumbeats as well as clapping and ululation.

After a close examination of the congregation characterized by a moment of total silence, the clergyman makes a revolution with his folded' fists shouting at the top of his voice" PRA—PRA—PRA—ISE THE LORD". In unison the congregation respond Amen while others add phrases like Yes! *Ashindwe*, Hallelujah and thank you lord!

The clergyman then reads a verse in the Holy Book, which talks about how difficult it is for a rich man to enter the Kingdom of Heaven. He emphasizes the verse by condemning those people who live in glass and marble houses yet the House of the Lord is only made of iron sheets.

"Yes, the Bible says in the gospel of Mark 10:25: It is easier for a camel to go through the eye of a needle than for a rich man to enter the Kingdom of God". He concludes his sermon.

The preacher's sermon is rightly timed in that among the congregation that Sabbath day are the local member of parliament and a handful of other tycoons from the vicinity. His long sermon is delivered in such a manner that the parishioners are made to believe without any ray of doubt that it is better to be poor and inherit the kingdom of heaven than to be rich and burn ad-infinitum in hell.

This was going to be good; Tito thought and tried his best to get as comfortable as possible. But the preacher went on and on about the coming of Jesus and how all sinners would get to hell and burn and burn and burn. It did not scare Tito, he had heard all about hell and he was prepared for the fire. Every night before he fell asleep he would ask God, whom he didn't know so well, to take him at night so that he would arrive in hell drunk as a fish. This way, he would be too drunk to feel the heat. Unfortunately, he always woke up to the same world. And if booze belonged to Satan, well that made things even better. More booze, more intoxication, less heat. So he just switched off from the sermon and waited for the show stopper the miracles. How interesting this Sunday was going to be.

He was jolted back to the present by the singing of the people and he realized that the preacher was calling out to every one to give their offerings to God. There were some ushers moving in the crowd and collecting large sums of money. They kept going back to the pulpit to pour the money into bigger bags and came back into the crowd for more money. Tito envied God for all this. If all this money belonged to Him, then He sure was a rich guy. When it seemed like everyone had given, of course, except Tito, the preacher asked for all those who had any problems and needed miracles, to raise their hands. He further asked everyone to close their eyes real tight and not to attempt to open them. If they did, he warned, they would see God and this was an abomination! Given the force with which he said this, I believe nobody dared to keep their eyes open. Well not everyone. At least one man who was perched on a tree and who had come just to witness miracles did not see any reason to be afraid. He reasoned that he did not need a miracle but he needed to *see* one because he had always wondered how God did it. This was his chance and nothing was going to stop him from watching God at his work. And Tito's eyes remained open.

The prayers began with a lot of shouting and crying and the Man of God invited God to come down and heal His people. Tito's heart started beating faster and faster in anticipation. His eyes shifted to the baskets into which the ushers had been putting the money. He expected God to take His money before offering His services but something quite unusual happened; there was movement from behind the stage and since everyone was busy shouting, they couldn't hear what was going on. Several strong men picked the big bags and got ready to leave with them as if the money belonged to them. Tito wanted to shout at them to stop and to alert the preacher that God's money was being stolen but just then the Man of God opened his eyes and began chanting, "God is here, God is here, God is here." And the crowd shouted louder and louder. The preacher went to his boys and gestured to them for a while before ushering them out of the stage to a waiting car.

So when the prayers ended, a good number of people ran on to the pulpit with testimonies about how God had healed them and taken away their burdens. They even testified about how they had felt God's presence. Tito slowly climbed down the tree and also went to give his testimony and this is what he said, "I was on top of the tree but I did not close my eyes when the Man of God told us to do so. I am glad I did not because today I, Tito, saw God. He was right here and he took his money and talked to preacher. God was here and I saw him."

Nobody believed Tito but he still tells his story to anyone who cares to listen. I believe him though and that is why I decided to tell you this remarkable story as told to me by Tito himself.

TORN ASUNDER

Maximilla's happiest day was when she got married to Jackson at the Cathedral. It was refreshing to see so many faces turning up to agree unanimously that Jack was now hers and she was his. She had never thought, not even once, that Jack would take her hand in marriage. So when he proposed to her just one month ago, she thought her ears had filled with boerewoers and that she was having selective auditory perceptions. *Will you marry an old pair of socks like this one?* Perhaps not in so many words. Soon she was witnessing the preparations, the helter-skelter. And in no time showers of confetti were assailing her as women ululated and men whistled. So they got married on that Saturday of the month of February. Jack bought for her a rocking chair for a gift which she would find waiting for her in their new home. And so the vows were pronounced at the Cathedral with Maximilla's moist eyes fixed at Jack all the time, even as he pronounced the "I do" therefrom ending all her days of anxiety in the elusive search for a genuine man among hordes of fakes. How her friends would envy her, how she would become the talk of the neighborhood. How a simple country girl charmed her way into the heart of a lofty and opulent Prince.

Following a very successful wedding and a small reception held at the Calypso, the newlywed couple took a rented boat and headed to California beach where they would spend a wonderful honeymoon. Of course it would be wonderful since Jack had just received a fully paid leave and wisely shut out all links with the public. But Maximilla would write letters to her folks back home pretty often. She would also send post cards of California those of Jack, a happy, smiling, contented man. Here he was eating a salmon, there he was riding a bicycle, here and there again, her swimming in the Ocean. The sandy beach, gulls. Joy and serenity to the very last whistle.

Active life resumed upon their return. Maximilla had regained some fists of fat due to the honeymoon. Now it was time for her to see to it that the extras were comfortably inculcated in her work routines. She looked for a job and found one at Sana laundry and dry cleaners. She promptly settled into her routines, morning, noon and night. Jack maintained his job at the stock exchange. Maximalla's endeavours at making Jack a happy husband were apparently bearing fruit by the day. She considered herself a competent wife. In the old days, competency would be measured in terms of the ripeness of the *ugali* cooked by the wife, a feat that either won or lost her a husband. Okay, those days had passed by, but still she mused that if she was to judge her performance by such standards of tradition she would definitely pass in flying colors. Besides, she was able to save out of her income, a sign of good economy. Who was to tell? One day she would surprise Jack with some exotic present. If she had not known happiness before, if she had not come any closer to bliss, now she did. Her accumulation of calories did not stop with the end of the honeymoon. A month into their married lives revealed an increase of significant chunks. Jack did not seem to mind these changes. Asked to comment on her new bigger figure, he would unanimously support the idea of weight gain and assure her that a flank of fat on both sides complemented her roles as a mother in the making. What about her bosom? Her arms? Hips?

Later she would discover, much to her chagrin and sorrow, that appearances blinded people to slavery and systematic self- destruction. She would discover that men could change to other things, at the blink of an eye. These lessons that did not come on a silver platter, to a simple village girl born in the escarpments of Sibilo where life was summarized to peasantry activities day after market day. Life was a funny thing, where one learnt by doing. There were no pilot schemes to be set aside before an idea was filtered into the mainstream. One perfected one's instincts through practice and experience of past failures, disappointments and delusions. Finally, when her romance faded like a *mtumba* jeans, life for the couple became a vicious cycle, a routine of chores and burdens like gears that miss oiling and begin to emit ear-piercing shrieks.

One day Maximilla came across, quite by accident, a small folded note from Jack's pocket as she was in the process of ironing his shirt. Following the squeeze and the tugs that the garment had endured during the washing, the orthography was now faded and the material delicate. But yes it was most clearly a *lettre doux*, a love note. It was signed Joan in clear print at the very bottom. Asking him about the note during the evening meal produced an unsightly response, partly accidental. He brusquely wiped his mouth with the serviette and pushed the unfinished plate away, which in its jolt disturbed an adjacent bowl of soup resulting in a chaotic tumble. Luckily, the soup was tepid, otherwise the couple would have had to spend many days in hospital suffering from burns of second degree nature. Having majestically walked out on her and her inquisitions and closed the door with a reverberating bang, the subject of notes and other related suspicions was officially closed. Much later in the night he would return to the lounge to find her asleep on the couch, sprawled helplessly like a shroud, popcorns scattered all over the furnishing. Dried tears on both her cheeks indicated that she had taken a good weep prior to her now serene composure punctuated by an occasional hiccup. He scooped her off the couch spilling more popcorns dotting her chest and carried her, with her arms dangling to another room. He also took the packet of popcorns and laid it beside her head where she would find it first thing when she awoke, lest he be accused of sharing her popcorns with Joan while she slept. He returned to switch on the television and slumped tiredly on the same couch. Clearly, he had overreacted, an exaggerated show of irritation that pointed to his guilt. Now, about this note that was threatening his peace. How could he explain to her that there were no extra marital affairs going on? And yet Maximilla had grown so cold lately, as if her love for him had faded away now. So much for faded loves and bygones, he had a rough day at work and therefore was in tough shape. He needed tranquility.

Although they did not openly talk about it, yet they felt that Joan's intrusion could turn out to be disastrous to their marriage, especially since they both themselves came from unstable family backgrounds. For example, both of their parents had had a divorce at one stage or the other of their lives. Maximilla suggested outright that Jack should leave his current job if only to keep off that slut of a secretary. She supported her point of view with a citation from the Bible, somewhere within the Book of Proverbs where one was urged to run like a deer when confronted by others of the opposite sex out to manipulate them to ruin.But it was incredible to think that in a couple of weeks Jack would actually leave Maximilla to cohabit openly with his secretary, resulting in a complete heartbreak for Maximilla. He would not listen to her pleas to come back. Days turned into weeks. It rained, it shined. Night and day. Hours of haunting loneliness. Seconds that felt like eons in their sluggish passing.

Finally, Jack returned one Sunday morning not to pursue any other business but to collect his files and other belongings. Maximilla was in the kitchen. When she saw him enter she would have jumped with joy. But this was not to be, especially after she saw the cold look in his face. She stared inquisitively. He did not give her much room to start staring competition. He shuffled his feet and went to the other room, picking things and stuffing them inside his grey travelling bag. Sounds of falling objects came from the kitchen as if she was inviting devils and fiends to witness the events and then seeking their hand to bring the house down. Clearly she was becoming enraged with every second passing. Names like Lucifer and monster were being summoned and Jack was unsure whether they were being addressed to him or to the walls of the kitchen. Wishing to escape before he witnessed something unsightly, Jack hurried up with the shuffling of files and books. Unfortunately for him, he could not avoid meeting her at the door as he was leaving, with the bag strapped to his back.

"What? You are leaving again? You know we have to talk, let me have a word with you please." She blurted, "What is this disrespect about? Living with a slut instead of your loyal wife at home? Tell me how to explain this....this embarrassment, this childishness to my parents. Tell me!" "Milla, listen okay? ...(he called her by a pet name that no one found very romantic then) I have nothing to explain...I need to stay away to reorganize priorities...." "Priorities my foot! You devil!" she exploded.Why was he trying to remain humble to a disrespectful and bullying woman when he had already made a stand, pray? "Okay you asked for it. Now just get out of my way before I do something uncivilized. And do not ever think that I can change my mind. If this is your idea of a conventional wifey husby *tete a tete*, then I think you would better revisit your horoscopes or something, otherwise to me you are just as 'slutly' as Joan. Only with all that fat and jelly of yours, you are a bigger slut than she is." Well, that did it. The look that his wife gave him, calm and cold and indifferent, was enough to reveal the venom underneath.

She lifted the metallic ladle and brought it down in a vicious swish on his balding head. The resulting impact produced a dull tonk that shook his entire skelton system. Funny that she had been wielding the weapon all the time yet he could not notice it. Now, he realized that he was being assaulted. The bag strapped on him became an immediate drawback to resistance. Obviously she was overstepping liberties. Another attack caught him across the lips and stung like the sting of a wasp. His bag fell in a heavy stomp making huge sweeps across the air. At one point the ladle broke and she had to remove her left shoe in order to extend the violence. He knew she would kill him if given the chance. She would zap him in cold blood and still continue with her mortal endeavours long after chopping his flesh to minced meat. He left her and just ran out for dear life. And so began her days of emptiness and nights of cold. Unanswered questions assailed her poor mind. On Thursday, quite on impulse, she went to see him at the workplace. He was not in but someone else was. Joan. And for the first time she met the woman who had so cruelly stolen her husband. Seeing her exquisite beauty and fragile charm, like that of a newborn baby, she knew why he had left her. She instantly grasped the reason behind the chemistry, behind his much- trumpeted departure. Joan paraded the figure that often found audience on magazine covers, tabloids and in television advertisements. Every time she talked to a client, responding to an enquiry, she telescoped her thin neck in a most comely manner. Compared to Joan, Maximilla looked like a tomboy, a tramp, an obese. A particularly well-dressed client actually dared to lean forward and reward her cuteness with a slight kiss on the cheek to which Joan thanked with professional courtesy.

Maximilla returned to her shell feeling flustered and spent. She no longer felt useful to Jack in the state she was in. She simply left his office. On several rash occasions she would pick the kitchen knife ready to slash her plump wrists and bleed herself to death. Mercifully, this did not occur. Weeping became her middle name, procrastination her constant preoccupation. She developed a phobia from looking at herself in the mirror. Every time she caught a glimpse of her image reflected on a shiny surface, mirror, windowpane, pans, water...she froze at the image that jumped at her. A hag. Later on, upon learning of what had happened, her mother sent her a family friend to stay with her to curb her loneliness. The mother had also undergone a similar experience at some point of her life.

"Men have this strange behaviour at some stage in their lives when they realise that life is not eternal and so they develop an urge to have it all before things start to depreciate. Maximilla's mother counseled her, "Before grey hair starts to show, before energy begins to wane." "They realise and become acutely aware of their imminent impotence. Men fear that at one point in time, their wives will find them weak and "womanly" and that they risk being abandoned. Therefore they see the best way to avoid losing face by being the first to go on the offensive. So child, do not worry about your present predicament. Okay, we have AIDS lurking in our midst and people should take care and all, but I assure you that your marriage is only going through a temporary phase, and it will pass."

So Maximilla and her mother spent their days and nights. Maximilla went to work every morning and returned home exhausted, mostly due to psychological stress. Her favourite songs on the radio became those of feminist tones like Destiny's Child and Kelly Price. Jack was making an effort to settle down with Joan in an apartment. He was doing a good job of it. Life was apparently getting on smoothly. Jack was planning to leave the country with Joan once his divorce procedures were through. He was lounging one afternoon in the makeshift study next to the ventilator, just relaxing and swaying his arms in circles. A few minutes later, he became drowsy and fell asleep. Then he had the dream.

He was driving his van, coming home. Maximilla would be waiting for him. She would remove his coat, give him a massage and prepare him a hot dinner. On the road to his house he was going at a hundred miles an hour. A flat and practically deserted highway. Suddenly a truck appeared out of nowhere. It veered toward him. He swerved off the road. A blinding flash followed by a tumbling noise. Later on, he was limping helplessly heading toward home, he could see the house afar. Later still, he was banging at the door calling Maximilla's name, urgently. No one opened the door. Profound silence. He limped around the house to find the kitchen door ajar.

"Maximilla! Milla" he croaked, strutting across one room after another in futile search for his absent wife. Up and down, helter-skelter, Hickory-dickory, humptily-dumptily. He found nothing but an empty, abandoned house. His search, fervent and persistent, revealed nothing. He overturned furnishings, objects of art big and small. He overcame all corners, righted all skews, upturned all possible hoods and coverables. Having searched every nook and corner and having found nothing, but a void, he decided to look in the shed.

The woman he found there, hanging by a thick cable, strangled and very much a corpse, with eyes bulging out of their sockets and a strange nose twisted and suppressed was not Maximilla. He pushed the stiff body to one side feeling the decaying skin crawl and tear. He took a closer look. It was fearfully thin, the body. And the chest was an aggressive protuberance. He had visions afar of some devils playing dangerous and malicious tricks on him, carving strange masks of people close to him and inviting him, luring him to witness their cannibalistic rituals. But his shunted visions became short-lived, mortally severed when straight at his face, still held within the corpse's small finger appeared the glimmer of their wedding ring. And then it was all over the shed. It spinned and danced and jiggled and ping ponged. It sang to him and embraced him. It did the *mwomboko* and the *Kwasa kwasa*. It was all over him, all stretched about the semi darkness. Small bits, large chunks. Strings, loops, curves, coils, knots, all shining and filling with colour of gold. Voices from the horizon, choirs, confetti and vows, thoughts of marriage, eternal dedication....

When he finally took the decisive steps and took the cold, stiff crooked arm into his hand and looked up at those bulging balls of cornea, incredibly bulky viewed in totality, eyes that used to be slits of allure and romantic appeal, now grotesque and hundredfold, he understood. The ring was floating around the shed because his eyes were filled with tears.

"Jack! Jack! What is the matter, boy? You are drenched in sweat. You have been dreaming?" Joan was shaking his shoulder urgently. He woke up and yawned. He looked confusedly around him, wiping his face. He looked at Joan again. He looked at his pale hands. He rotated his head and saw the ventilator, humming in rhythm to the beat of his heart. His pale hands again. Sweat.

"I am going back, Joan! I've got to go. Going home. *Adieu, Joan! Farewell! Au Revoir!*" just like that, and he was out of the chair, heading for the door.

Normally, when people planned to make a journey, perhaps to distant places, they took time to organize and reschedule. It was only in extreme circumstances, very uncommon, that a man just woke up one day and headed for the mountains or the wilderness or some such impulsive pursuits. This one was one of those rare occurrences when Jack hobbled mechanically towards the exit.